FOR HIRE

The Apartment Manager Series

ERIN HUSS

velvet morning
press

Published by Velvet Morning Press

ISBN-13: 978-0692721803
ISBN-10: 0692721800

Cover design by Ellen Meyer and Vicki Lesage
Author photo by Ashley Stock

Got a vacancy on your bookshelf?
Check out the hilarious

Apartment Manager Series

I hereby dedicate this book to:

Natalie, Noah, Ryder, Emma and Fisher

for motivating me daily by asking,
"Are you done with that thing yet?"

PART ONE

Chapter 1

Cambria

"You what?" I yelled over the whistling of the espresso machine. "I don't think I heard you right." Bart, my boss, was of a certain age (that age being eighty-five). He had a low, grumbly voice that had grown grumblier over the years.

"I said, I decided to sell," he repeated, raising his voice half an octave.

I used the back of my hand to push Einstein (my nickname for the dark, unruly hair springing from my head) out of my face and placed his vanilla latte on the counter. "Sell what?"

Waiting behind him, Ms. Low-Fat Cap began tapping her Prada on the tiled floor, with lips pursed and a "shut the hell up and let her make my drink!" glare locked and loaded and pointed at the back of Bart's sparsely haired head, as if about to fire laser beams from her eyeballs. If there's one thing I had learned in my six years of managing a café, it was that people took their coffee seriously. Very seriously. Life or death seriously. I will literally kill you and your entire family if you don't steam my milk to 102 degrees seriously. It was much like dealing with Lilly on the brink of an epic toddler meltdown, except I could put her in timeout. Here, I had to smile and nod and duck as the "I said extra whip" mocha came flying at my head.

"Your drink is coming right up," I told her.

She stood up straighter and feigned obliviousness, placing her manicured hand over her chest as if saying *Oh me? I'm just patiently waiting.*

Sure you are.

"Cambria, listen," Bart pressed, with his business face on.

"Yes, sorry. What are you selling?"

"It's time to close this place up," he said with an unapologetic shrug. He arched his gray, bushy brows, making it difficult to tell if he was being serious or attempting an *I'm old so I can get away with it* bad joke. I found no humor when it came to my livelihood. Not when I was on my own with a toddler to feed and bills to pay and one of the many freckles dotting my face was a shade darker than the rest and needed to be looked at. Because if there's one thing more expensive than toddlers and bills, it's healthcare.

"You're telling me you're actually considering selling the café? No way. This is a joke," I decided, shaking my head. He'd opened Bart's Café in the sixties, never married, no kids, and he'd told me he planned on dying behind the bar doing what he loved. How could he die here if he didn't own it? He'd be hard-pressed to find a buyer willing to agree to those terms.

"I'm not selling the café. I'm selling the building. This is a large lot, and a strip mall would be really good for the community."

This is absurd. "Bart, it's Los Angeles. There's a strip mall next door. Someone is trying to bully you into selling again. The last thing we need is another nail salon and smoke shop. I told you, I'm in one hundred percent."

He groaned, placing an elbow on the counter, looking tired. "I signed the papers this morning."

"What?" I shrieked, dropping the pitcher of hot milk I was frothing. It hit the counter, knocking over the row of paper cups waiting to be filled, and splashed its contents down the front of my apron. The boiling two percent seeped through the thin fabric, turning the metal button and zipper of my jeans into an iron, branding "Mossimo" onto my pelvic region.

Certain situations are beyond profanity.

This was one of them.

Squealing and hopping around in agony, I managed to make it to the stock room before yanking my pants down to my ankles. The first aid kit was located in the office, a good seven-foot journey. *Too far.* Frantic, I hobbled to the fridge, grabbed a carton of soy milk and pressed it on my burning unmentionables.

The cool paperboard calmed the sting. I fell back against the wall and slid down to my butt, sighing the entire way. Mike, one of many part-time baristas, darted around the corner, saw me lying on the floor with my pants down, holding soy milk to my crotch, and quickly twirled around to face the opposite direction.

"Um... you OK, boss?" he asked, staring at the required safety signs covering the wall. I imagined his face was as red as the hair on his head.

Not a good day to sport my granny panties.

"Yeah, I should be fine," I answered through gritted teeth, lifting the tight elastic of my grannies to take a look at the damage. A shiny red line ran down my lower abdomen. Not too bad. No blisters, no blood. There would definitely be a scar—a small one that would blend in with the stretch marks.

First degree, I thought.

"OK, um," Mike stuttered, still staring at the Safety Guidelines as if his life depended on it. "Err... Bart is on the patio, and he said for you to come out and talk to him when you're finished."

Oh, that.

A scalding milk bath had a way of erasing all other troubles. If only for a moment. "Tell him I'll be out in a bit," I said, wincing as I readjusted the soy. I needed time to overthink the situation before I talked to Bart again.

Mike was all too eager to play messenger, dashing out into the morning crowd before the sentence had completely left my mouth.

Poor kid.

I rested my head on the wall and took a deep breath, allowing the new information to settle in like a bad infection. I felt furious and sad. Betrayed. Bart carelessly delivering the news wasn't a surprise. He avoided emotions like the stomach flu. Him selling the café though, that was a shock so big it felt as if a semi had just rolled over my chest.

Mad, I took it out on the fridge door, kicking it closed with my black Converse. This backfired when I caught a glimpse of my reflection in the mirror-like stainless steel. Einstein was pointing in every direction but south. My blue eyes were cushioned in red, puffy bags, and then there was the whole granny situation. I looked every bit the sixty-five years I felt, except I was twenty-eight.

I closed my eyes, wishing my life had a Refresh button. If it did, I would have selected pants *without* a zipper. I could have refreshed the day that Bart pulled me aside and told me he'd like to leave the café to me. He said he wanted Bart's to live on well after he was gone, and there was no one he trusted more than me. He provided information on deeds and bank accounts and tax forms. Doing it over, I still would have graciously accepted, but I wouldn't have banked my future on it. Or maybe got it in writing? Signed something? Not mentally designed business cards with "Owner" written below my name? Not have spent my own money on trinkets and artwork to spruce up the place?

Crap.

Determined to get answers, I charged out to the patio (after a quick, albeit awkward, aloe vera lather). Bart was in his usual spot, slouched in a plastic chair next to the parking lot. The patio was full with the regulars: Bob and his laptop, Chris and this week's girlfriend, Rachel and her Chihuahua. A group of women decked out in expensive tennis clothes chatting over lattes and taking pictures of the scones they were nibbling on.

I took the seat across from Bart, crossing my arms on the table, and studied the old man in front of me. The collar of his plaid shirt poked out from under his navy fleece, the one with the Dodger's emblem embroidered on the upper left breast. His ears looked longer and his face more creased. He had one hand resting atop a thick, unmarked, manila envelope.

I couldn't speak. I could only stare and wait. Then I remembered whom I was sitting with. Bart's viewpoint on communication was "why use words when a shrug will do?" Which is why I handled all personnel problems.

Not knowing what to say, I started with the obvious. "I'm here."

He took a sip of his latte. His face was momentarily masked in steam, leaving his brows and nose hairs glistening. "It's good foam," he finally said, staring at the cup, running his thumb over the Bart's Café logo printed on the sleeve.

I wasn't here to talk about foam, especially not after it burned my lady bits. "Why did you sell?" We needed to stop beating around the bush.

"I was made an offer I couldn't refuse."

"By who? The Godfather? You've had a lot of offers over the years you've managed to refuse. Why now? Why not give me a heads-up? Why after everything you said about how you wanted Bart's to live on forever? And if you were going to sell, why not give me the opportunity to at least make a bid? I've poured my soul into this place."

He let out a little moan and waved his hand, as if flicking away a tiny insect trying to fly up his nose. "It's too damn expensive to keep a business alive around here. You can buy a decent cup of coffee at the 76 Station. It's not worth throwing all your eggs into this basket. Assuming you have any saved up." If eggs were money, then no, I didn't have any reserved eggs. But I had good credit. That had to be worth loaner eggs. "It would go down eventually. I'd rather it go down on my watch."

Does he think he's doing me a favor?

"I want to retire and have some *big* adventures."

Guess not.

"Here." He slid the envelope across the table. "Last paychecks for everyone and a little something extra for yourself."

I stared at the envelope as if it were contagious, unable to conjure up the right words. Perhaps there weren't any. The papers had been signed. The situation had to be accepted. The café was closing. Bart was off to a big adventure. And I was a single mother with no college education, no job and burnt unmentionables.

"I'll let everyone know," I said, fidgeting with the string-tie on my employment coffin. "What do we do with… everything?" I waved my hand around, gesturing to the tables and the chairs and the umbrellas and all the other makeup of the company that had been serving the public since 1960.

He replied with a shrug.

"I'll let you handle it then," I said, my voice small as I

choked back a sob.

Bart squirmed—too many feelings happening. "Leave the keys on the desk. I'll take care of it. And… *thanks.*" He stood with more spring than I'd seen from him in years and nearly galloped to his…

What. The. Hell?

Parked in Bart's spot was a muscular yellow Mustang with chrome rims. RIMS. He'd been driving a brown Buick with missing hubcaps for decades. The baristas and I called it the Political Time Machine because he had a bumper sticker for every Republican presidential candidate since Nixon stuck on the trunk. Now he had a Mustang. A YELLOW Mustang.

This was bananas.

Bart revved the engine, causing Rachel's Chihuahua to take cover under the chair. He drove the muscle car just as he drove the Political Time Machine. Idling out of the space, rolling through the parking lot and out to oncoming traffic, cutting off a driver or two.

He was gone, and all I got was a measly "thanks" and his empty latte cup left on the table.

I grabbed the manila envelope and unwrapped the string keeping it closed. Inside were more envelopes, each with a barista's name and then, at the very back of the stack, were two for me. My name was spelled wrong and scribed in flowery, unfamiliar handwriting. I'd been handling payroll for the last year. It was hard to believe he managed to do all this without my knowing. The first was my last paycheck, paying me through the end of the month. Good. The next check would have to cover my rent and bills until I found another job. I ran my finger under the sealed flap, careful not to add a paper cut to my list of current maladies, pulled out the check and held it up, blinking hard at the numbers staring back at me.

Bart wasn't being figurative when he said a *little* something for me.

Chapter 2

Joyce

By the time Joyce Plummer, the onsite apartment manager, followed the power cords through the courtyard and into the first laundry room, Daniella and Carmen were already screaming and swearing and stamping their feet. Carmen, from Apartment 26, had a basket of dirty whites propped on one hip and a baby balanced on the other. Her mousy hair was tied in a knot, and she looked as if she'd been punched repeatedly in the face by insomnia. Daniella, on the other hand, looked rested and fresh and preened. Her dark hair curled into loose waves, and her face was painted on bright and thick.

If it came to blows, Joyce had her money on Daniella. She was a decade older and a foot shorter than Carmen, but she was scrappy. She once poured maple syrup into the rent collection box because she wasn't allowed to have a charcoal barbecue pit.

"You're an inconsiderate piece of dog crap!" Carmen yelled, readjusting her basket.

"Woof!" replied Daniella.

"I said crap, not dog! You're dog crap! Crap doesn't bark!"

A dirty sock went flying over Joyce's bright red hair and landed in the walkway. Rolling her eyes, she leaned against the doorjamb and pulled a pack of Marlboro Reds from her back pocket. Her hands shook as she pounded the fresh pack against her tiny palm. It was hard to know if the shakes were a byproduct of the arthritis or the stress of too many decades of property management. It could also be the nicotine. She was up to three packs a day.

Suddenly, it was raining dryer sheets.

Joyce remained unfazed. She'd seen everything. Three-in-the-morning emergency calls about poorly installed stripper poles. Residents who kept bed bugs as therapy pets. A hamster caught in the bathtub drain... Nothing shocked her any more.

So of course the quarreling women had little impact. Neither did the crockpot on top of the washing machine simmering what smelled like beef stew or the toaster oven on the second washer heating up Home Style Garlic Bread (as per the box on the ground next to the pool of Tide). Dirty spatulas and ladles were scattered on the counter along with a cutting board and a colander filled with sliced vegetables. Orange power cords were plugged into the outlets designated for the dryers, and ran across the room and out the door. The laundry room had been transformed into a kitchen and a generator, and it didn't take a detective to know why.

Daniella hadn't paid her electric bill.

Last time this happened, Joyce caught her in a vacant unit using the kitchen to prepare a four-course meal for her salsa instructor. Joyce was showing the apartment to a prospective tenant when she found Daniella massacring a Butterball with an electric knife. There were turkey gizzards and raw bits all over the newly glazed counters and salmonella juice dripping down the front of the cabinets.

This was before the accident, back when Joyce was capable of empathy. She hadn't come down too hard on Daniella, sympathetic to her financial hardships (and she had managed to rent the apartment regardless). Now, she just didn't give a damn any more.

With the cigarette balanced between her wrinkled lips, Joyce unsteadily brought the lighter up and ignited the end. She inhaled several times and blew out ringlets of smoke (a trick she'd been practicing), counting each one before it disappeared.

The room went quiet except for the ticking of the kitchen timer next to the crockpot. The two women stared at Joyce. Daniella's lips turned down in the corners as if she were a toad. Carmen dropped her laundry basket and used her free hand to cover her baby's mouth. Seven was the child's name. Joyce wasn't sure if it was a boy or a girl, or when prime numbers became first names. All she knew was Seven had a pair of big brown eyes that hurt her heart.

Damn.

She reached into her back pocket for the pack of Marlboro Reds, forgetting one was already pinched between her fingers.

"Joyce," Carmen said, coughing dramatically. "You can't smoke in public areas. Those things are cancer sticks."

Daniella bobbed her head in agreement.

Joyce scoffed. The entire country had gone wacko. Everyone felt they had a right to share their opinion on her habit, whether she asked for it or not. Even the billboard near the liquor store, the one displaying a picture of a smoldering cigarette with a shadow of a gun behind it, weighed in on the subject. *QUIT TODAY. SMOKING KILLS* it said in bold black lettering. Every

her finger. "You need, like, an ambulance or something?"

Joyce pushed her finger away. Nothing pissed her off more than pity. "I'm..." She cleared her airway once more. "Fine." She coughed into her fist and used the other hand to give Daniella the Three-Day Notice she had prepared earlier, when she had been sitting behind her desk and spotted Daniella hauling the crockpot into the laundry room.

Daniella pinched the paper between her thumb and forefinger. "What is this?"

"Shape up or cruise out." *Cough! Cough!* "And clean this up." *Cooouuugh!*

"What? You can't threaten to kick me out, Yoyce!"

"Looks like she just did," Carmen almost sang, pulling the basket of dirty whites back up on her hip. She cocked her head and flashed a smile, baring large teeth. "Now get all this out of here so I can do my laundry."

"Yeah, yeah, what she said," Joyce rasped in between coughs. She took the small step out of the laundry room and onto the walkway, pulling out a fresh cigarette as fast as her hands would allow and lit it.

Much better.

"Yoyce!"

Never mind.

Chapter 3

Cambria

I lived near LAX in a community I'd christened Crap-o-la Apartments. Crap-o-la was your average two-story seventies-inspired building with exposed stairwells and palm trees out front. There were weathered couches in the walkways, bars on the windows and beer cans shoved in the bushes. The one-bedroom apartments were 600 square feet of scratchy, vomit-colored carpet, with white walls and crap-colored tiles (hence the name).

The neighborhood, at best, was questionable. The overhead planes drowned out the numerous sirens, yet prompted the drunks coming from the bar on the corner to speak louder. The sidewalks never slept. And parking was nonexistent; tickets were simply an allotted monthly expense.

I had been scouting new apartments right before Bart's Café was torn down.

The only plus side of Crap-ol-a was the free babysitting from my next-door neighbors, Mr. and Mrs. Nguyen. Them watching my three-year old daughter, Lilly, was invaluable. Childcare is expensive. Residing in

Southern California is expensive. Existing is so damn expensive—and I felt every last cent of it.

I was surviving on unemployment and the measly severance Bart felt my years of service were worth (still a ~~little~~ lot bitter about that). I would not admit defeat though. The job market was dry, yes. But I was confident I'd be able to find employment worthy of my skills both as a manager and a strong, hardworking, independent woman.

"Cambria, would you say your ovaries are in good condition?"

"Excuse me?"

"Your ovaries, are they healthy?" my best friend, Amy, repeated from her spot at my table, hunched over the laptop. The light from the screen danced across her clear blue eyes and reflected off the splint holding her newly constructed nose together.

In the kitchen, I stood on my tiptoes to extricate the bottle of vanilla bean syrup from the top shelf. The colorful label was coated in a thin layer of dust, but the expiration date gave me the go-ahead. I twisted off the cap and eyeballed a tablespoon into each of our drinks. "I don't think I want a job that asks about my reproductive organs," I said, adding a splash more of syrup to my Dirty Diet Coke.

"Says here if you're between the ages of twenty-six and twenty-nine, you can get up to six thousand dollars if you try this new drug. You can do up to six injections." Her nasal voice was tinged with glee, almost giddy, as if she'd just discovered how to spin straw into gold. "Quick, what's six thousand times six?"

"Not enough to inject anything into my ovaries." I placed our drinks on the table and took a seat, moving Lilly's Elsa doll off the chair before I flattened it. "Is that the only new ad on Craigslist?"

"No, I Googled 'desperate for income' and this

clinical trial company came up. I personally don't think it's a bad idea. But you're only eligible while you're ovulating." She twisted her blond and purple streaked hair up into a bun. Even in sweats, a bandaged nose and makeup-less face, she still looked every bit the beautiful wannabe actress she was. "If you can handle a giant epidural needle, then you should be able to handle the nightly injections. The needle should be smaller. Says here the most common side effects are change in appetite, bloating and baldness."

I gave my best friend since third grade a *please stop talking* look.

"Cambria, it's not as if you like your hair. There's a reason you call it Einstein. Wigs are totally in right now. And just think about it like this: you're throwing away six grand every month. Poof! Gone."

"Fine!" If I didn't fake compliance, she'd be able to talk me into it. She was good at that. Convinced me into sporting an A-line bob once. It would complement your face, she told me. In the end, it looked like I had a Pomeranian glued to my head. "Bookmark the page, and I'll look into it," I lied, then took a quick sip of my drink. The beautiful blend of calories danced across my taste buds, easing the budding stress in my shoulders. Sugar had a way of making everything better. If only I had the same response to cauliflower, maybe I'd be able to squeeze my butt back into my pre-Lilly wardrobe.

"When's your next ovulation date?" Amy asked, scratching her nose carefully with her pinky finger.

"Let's circle back to menstruation. In the meantime, I have to finish filling this out." I held up an application for a shift supervisor position at Coffee, Tea and Smoothies!, a chain I despised under normal circumstances (their smoothies tasted like Dimetapp), but they were hiring, and I was wanting. "They need four references, and I'm stuck. I can only think of one."

"Who?"

"Tom."

Amy chuckled silently, as to not disturb the new snout. "What did you write? Thomas Dryer, guy-I-still-pine-over slash friend-zoner slash baby-daddy slash pro-*bone*-ing everyone but me, attorney at law?"

"Shh!" I scolded, jerking my head in the direction of the living room, where Lilly was hanging upside-down on the couch with a Barbie in each little hand, her hazel peepers fixated on *The Mickey Mouse Clubhouse*. The ends of her dark curls brushed the carpet as she giggled in joyful obliviousness—exactly as it should be. As a child, as an *only* child, I was privy to all my parents' marital and post-marital troubles. Determined not to subject Lilly to the same damaging animosity, I was careful not to talk about Tom in a negative light around her. Not that we were ever married. We never even dated. We went from "would you like a drink?" to "crap, I'm late!" to "we should just be friends." He's still a great dad though, and at the end of the day that's all that matters.

"Oh, oh, oh!" Amy bounced around in her chair as if she had to pee. "I've got it. The People Perfect Party Palace Place is always looking for characters. I know you hate that kind of stuff, but you wear a costume for an hour, and you get compensation *and* tips. I made two hundred bucks as Cinderella two weeks ago."

"I'd rather perform my own colonoscopy."

"That's... *kinky*."

"I'm not *that* desperate yet. It's only been a month. Plus, we moved to L.A. so *you* could become an actor—not me." I tagged along for the ride because that's how our friendship worked.

Amy gave me the same look I gave Lilly when she refused to try her vegetables. "You wouldn't have to act. They don't need princesses. All you'd have to do is wear a costume and stand and pose for pictures. No one would even see your face."

"I'll think about it." *Not a chance.*

"What about becoming an Uber driver?"

"My car doesn't qualify." It was an old Civic, scratched, faded paint, made a clicking noise when I turned. Had a lot of character—too much for Uber apparently.

"Hey, why are we even stressing about this?" Amy asked, closing my laptop. "Didn't you have a job interview today?"

Ugh.

I nodded.

It hadn't gone well.

The ad called for an experienced restaurant manager with a dedication to customer service. A café was almost like a restaurant, and as far as customer service went, I was devoted. The Toil Tavern was located in Culver City, had decent Yelp reviews and according to Google, catered to a high-end professional crowd. I showed up in a pink pencil skirt, matching blazer and a white shirt underneath. Fake golden studs adorned my ears, and Einstein was twisted and secured to my scalp with a claw clip—my interpretation of high-end professional.

The building was black stone with no windows and a concrete fire pit near the front entrance. The flames dancing behind the polycarbonate protection of the fire pit gave the building a naughty vibe—and I liked it. I imagined the atmosphere more alluring in the pitch-black of midnight as opposed to the bright mid-day glare I was experiencing it in. Thus the "dusk till dawn" hours kept.

After a quick knock on the red velvet door, I had stepped back and waited as the nerves began clawing at my stomach, picking at my confidence. The last job I'd interviewed for was as a barista at Bart's seven years ago, where the main point of concern was my hours of availability. I was out of practice. I should have looked up interview pointers. I should have watched YouTube videos. I should have worn thinner clothing.

Note to self: Wear three layers of deodorant to job interviews.

I yanked on my collar and leaned down, willing cool air down my shirt as the nerve-sweat pumped from my pits at fire-hydrant-speed.

Of course, this is when the door opened.

A woman twice my height, half my weight and with a quarter of the clothes on stood before me. Her black shorts hugged her perfectly curved butt and her shirt clung to her double-d's, stopping at her ribcage as to better show off the diamond in her bellybutton. I had no idea what color her hair was. I couldn't stop staring at the cleavage. I'd never felt so overdressed in my life.

"Um, I'm here for a job interview," I said, stammering, still pulling at my collar. Between the nerves and the heat and the flames and the red door, it felt as if I were standing at the gates of Hell.

The gatekeeper, a.k.a. Kimmy, per the nametag pinned alarming close to her right nipple, regarded me, batting her goopy lashes.

"My name is Cambria Clyne," I offered, feeling beads of sweat slithering down my face, carving grooves into my makeup.

"Oooohh," Kimmy purred, while twirling her hair between two fingers (the hair being blond with blue tips—finally noticed). "That makes sense, the manager position. Come on in." She turned on her ten-inch platforms and granted me entrance with a wave of her hand.

The fiery theme continued into the interior—red velvet booths with dark marble tabletops. Golden frames showcasing abstract art hung where windows should be. The walls were covered in black wallpaper dazzled in gold and silver specs. A large circular bar with high-backed red barstools took up the center of the restaurant with an empty space reserved for dancing.

In the bright florescent lighting it looked like a glorified Red Robin. I imagined during operating hours the lighting was dimmed and the scuffed flooring was hidden, giving the room an "I'm here with my two mistresses" kind of vibe.

I followed Gatekeeper Kimmy as she pranced the way. We stopped at a booth near the back, occupied by a man who I assumed to be Cash, the general manager who would be conducting my interview. He had slicked dark hair, large brown eyes and a thin mustache. So thin, it looked as if he'd drawn it on with a Sharpie.

If this was Hell, and Kimmy was the Gatekeeper, then Cash was the Ruler of the Underworld. And he very much looked the part in his black suit and shiny red lapel.

Gulp.

I slid onto the bench, placing my bag on my lap, hoping the weight would keep my knees from shaking. No such luck.

"You're Kelly?" Cash asked, smoothing his barely-there mustache with his thumb and forefinger.

"No, I'm Cambria, Master Sir."

Master Sir?

He appeared not to hear, or not to care, or perhaps he was used to being addressed as such. "OK, let's get started." Master Sir Cash didn't bother removing his eyes from the table. "Tell me about your last restaurant, Kelly."

"It's, um, Cambria. That's my name. Came-Bree-Ah. And I managed a café for almost six years until it closed recently."

His right brow twitched upward. "The last place you managed closed down?"

"Oh, no, I mean, yes, but it closed because the owner sold the building. Not because of anything I did wrong. Hejustdidn'twanttobeinbusinessanymorethat'sallcrossmy heart." The words shot out of my mouth so fast, they bypassed the Filter Station.

Note to self: Think first. Speak second.

"You know, I don't normally dress this conservatively," I announced, for no apparent reason. *Crap. THINK first!*

Master Sir Cash lifted his hand and snapped his fingers. Out of nowhere, Gatekeeper Kimmy appeared with a bottle of Bling H2O. After she poured the expensive liquid into a glass of ice, she scurried back to her post, waiting to be summoned again.

With his pinky finger extended, he took a sip. His movements slow, as if he were underwater. "Let me ask you, Kelly, do you believe this interview is going well?"

"I'm sorry, what?"

"This interview, do you believe it's going well?" he repeated, still addressing the tabletop.

Is this going well?

What kind of question is that?

Obviously, it could have been going better. Or worse, like I could have forgone the jacket hiding my pit stains. I'd already dumped a gallon of sweat into my outfit, which was going to make it difficult to return the following day as planned.

Master Sir Cash cleared his throat in an "I don't really have anything in my throat I just want you to hurry up" kind of way.

I sat up straighter. After a moment of deliberation, I went with, "I'm a much better employee than I am an interviewee." Truer words never spoken.

"That's nice... I think we're done here," he said while gathering the papers and pounding them into an orderly stack. He shoved the pile into a leather binder and exited the booth without another word.

No, no, no.

"Hold on." I scooted down the red plastic covering,

the sweat making it difficult to slide off the bench easily. I spilled onto the floor in a sweaty mess of Marshalls' finest apparel, spewing the contents of my bag. Great.

Using my forearm, I swept my belongings back in and struggled upright. "I ran a busy café for six years," I blurted out, speaking to the back of Cash's head as he strolled toward the bar. "I handled payroll, scheduling, tips, inventory and more than fifteen employees. I am the hardest worker you'll ever meet!"

He froze mid-step. Gatekeeper Kimmy propped a hand on her hip and watched with an *OMG* gaping expression.

Cash spun around with a surprised face on, as if I had just snuck up behind him and yelled, "Boo!" The heels of his shiny Oxfords clacked across the floor, slowly, echoing through the empty restaurant, until our toes met. His close proximity was unnerving. I tried not to squirm. He smelled like scotch and roses.

He studied my face with his big eyes, creasing his brow in deep deliberation before declaring, "I like you."

I felt like asking why, but decided to go with, "Thanks?"

He leaned back and tapped his chin with his finger. "I don't think you'd do well here. You do that nervous chatty thing. Not good. Wouldn't work. If you're interested, we're hiring at our sister location. You'd start off on the floor, of course, but it pays well, and the tips are excellent. There's plenty of room for advancement. Have you heard of The Palace?"

"Yes, of course I have." *Nope, never.*

He nodded, pleased. "I believe this may work," he decided. "Come with me, and I'll introduce you to the team."

Eager for employment, I followed him through a pair of double-swing doors and into the kitchen. It was empty, aside from the barely pubescent boy pushing boxes into the freezer. We walked past a door marked "Office" and another door marked "Security." Then, through another door and out to the alleyway we went. The narrow passage was big enough for a few bags of trash, a single Dumpster and the two homeless men who were rummaging through it.

We arrived at a chipped and dented silver door, etched in graffiti. A sign warning passers-by about the video surveillance used "24/7" hung sideways by a single nail.

As soon as the door opened, the delightful aroma of a deep fryer hard at work filled my nostrils. *These are my kind of peeps.* I trailed Cash though another double-swing door. The loud thumping of music drowned the hustle of the kitchen. The floor vibrated with the heavy bass, and the lighting darkened. He pushed open another set of doors, and we stepped into… BOOBS!

They were everywhere.

They were bouncing across the stage.

They were twirling around a pole.

They were gliding across the room with a serving tray.

The club was dark and musky. A geometric display of neon lights lit up the ceiling, and the furniture glowed orange and yellow under black lights. Two small stages flanked the long runway down the middle of the room with a pole at the end.

My emotions hovered somewhere between mortified and flattered.

"This is Ginger," Cash shouted over the Keisha club mix, introducing the woman at his side. Her auburn hair was sleeked into a bun, and her shorts were pink, and her stilettos were pink, as were her pasties—same color as my outfit. We were practically Pepto twins.

"H-h-hi, I'm Cambria."

"What?" yelled Ginger, leaning in close. She smelled

like pot.

"I said my name is... *ugh!*" I made some sort of strangled sound and rocked back on my heels, nearly tumbling over.

BART!

Bart stood up from a table, his shirt unbuttoned and his pants on crooked and his... *No! No!* I shook my head, trying to unsee what I was seeing.

"I didn't catch that, love," Ginger said into my ear.

"Um, um, um." My lips felt numb and my mind blank. "Um... my name is... Kelly. It's Kelly."

Ginger followed my gaze to Bart and the goofy grin spread across his face as he giddily followed a woman into a private room. "You know Bart?" she asked.

I shook my head *no* but said, "Yaiucka." Whatever that means.

"He's one of our regulars. Very generous. Especially if you are," she explained with a wink.

Gross. "Where's your restroom?"

"What?" She leaned in close.

"Your restroom! Where is it? I... um... gotta *go*. Too much to drink this morning," I said, as if peeing required an explanation.

"Past stage two, Love."

"Thank you!" I hurried past stage two, past the door marked "Restroom" and the door marked "Private Show" and the door marked "Champagne Room" and through the door marked "Emergency Exit." Running to my car as fast as my Payless pumps would take me. Cringing.

If someone wants to strip, fine. If an old man wants a lap dance, go for it. To each his or her own. I only wished I hadn't witnessed Bart's *BIG* adventure.

Again, certain situations are beyond profanity.

This was one of them.

Chapter 4

Joyce

Joyce scratched her head with her cigarette-free hand while staring at the twin mattress floating in the pool. The fitted sheet, somehow still on, was frayed and holey and a curious shade of yellow, with *"this is a mattress"* scrawled across it in marker. In case there was any confusion.

This had Kevin written all over it.

Literally.

He was a labeler. He said he did it for Joyce's benefit, you know, because she was old.

One time, he punched a hole in the laundry room wall, then wrote "here is a hole" with an arrow pointing to the hole in question.

"He has a *disability*," his mother had said when she moved him in. He appeared to be an average nineteen-year-old kid at the time. Although Joyce understood special needs weren't always visible. Her own Josh had his troubles, never looked people in the eyes and kept to himself. Doctor said he was "special"—and he was. He was very special and smart. Earned a PhD from Stanford in Bioengineering and used his fancy degree at a biotech company in the Valley, formulating medicine for chronic illnesses. Joyce took every opportunity to brag about it.

No one elaborated as to what Kevin's diagnosis was, nor did Joyce ask. In addition to owning the building Joyce managed, Kevin's parents owned half a dozen other communities across Los Angeles County, all managed by Elder Property Management (the small management company she worked for). Didn't seem like a good idea to pry.

After all, how difficult could he really be?

Fast-forward twenty years, and Kevin was perfectly summed up in an old nursery rhyme, the one about the little girl with a curl in the middle of her forehead Joyce used to recite to Josh.

When he was good,
he was very good indeed.
But when he was bad,
he was playing his saxophone in the middle of the night on his patio wearing nothing but socks.

Or however it went.

Everyone knew Kevin had been sent to live there for many reasons, and none of them had anything to do with a "disability." Still, meddling wasn't her style. She stayed out of his hair unless forced to intervene... those "intervenences" becoming more regular as of late. His file now took up two long cabinets.

At one time, she thought about compiling Kevin's incident reports and turning them into a novel—*The Man-Child Chronicles* she'd call it.

Bob had laughed when she told him. "If we wouldn't both get fired and sued for millions, I'd say go for it."

"You're probably right," she had replied, disappointed. Bob had spent five decades as her husband, four as an English teacher and one as a maintenance man. He knew what he was talking about.

Still, an apartment manager can dream.

Blowing out a cloud of smoke, Joyce moved to the edge of the pool. The tips of her white Hush Puppies hovered over the water as she surveyed the situation. *This isn't good.* Using the end of the pool skimmer, she poked at the mattress a few times to see if it would easily budge. No luck.

At least I tried.

Content with her effort, she shuffled the skimmer back to its spot on the fence, slid another cigarette between her lips, and headed back to the office—her sanctuary.

When she first started, the community averaged a thirty percent vacancy rate, high for a forty-unit building, especially one in a desired Los Angeles neighborhood. Why was the occupancy so low? Easy, the lobby was decorated in oranges and browns with clunky metal folding chairs. It reminded her of the waiting room at Bob's proctologist. In an apartment building, the front lobby is a direct reflection of the time and care management is willing to provide, and, if anything, it should say, "Welcome home" not "bend and cough."

Joyce spent weeks redecorating on the tight budget provided. This was before Pinterest and blogs and YouTube. She pored through magazines and interior design books, and took note of the décor on her favorite television programs. She and Bob painted, hung wallpaper, installed new lights and a ceiling fan, and put in new carpet, new tiles and new furniture. The lobby and office were transformed from seventies blah to early nineties ta-da!

Everything from the teal carpet to the bright floral armchairs to the dried eucalyptus branches hung above the overstuffed peach couch was timeless, so she thought. Attached to her apartment, the office and lobby were the only places she could go that didn't require too much walking, and didn't require the use of a car, and didn't hold too many painful memories. If only Joyce could smoke in there, she'd never leave.

Back in the office, Joyce took a seat behind her desk, intending to script the incident report (the tale of the yellow mattress), when the morning newspaper stole her attention. The plastic covering was still intact, which meant the crossword puzzle had yet to be solved. This must be done before work could resume.

You know, priorities.

The door chimed. Andy, a stout thirty-something with bird-like facial features, appeared at the counter, the one separating the enclosed office from the lobby. He cleared his throat, a wet, scratchy sound, and then belched into his fist, because saying "hello" was evidently not an option.

"Can I help you?" Joyce asked, annoyed. A five-letter word for *unitary* was all that stood between her and the satisfaction of completing a crossword puzzle.

Andy cleared his throat again, fidgeting with the "ring for service" bell next to the brochures. Joyce rose and met him at the counter. In a previous life, back when she gave a damn, she would have escorted Andy to the couch, eager to help with whatever was causing him to burp and sweat like a whore in a minister... or chapel... or however that saying went.

"Get on with it," Joyce urged, yanking the bell out of his hand before he broke it.

"Well... I'm having a problem with one of my neighbors."

"Kevin?"

"No."

"Silvia?"

"No."

"Daniella?"

"No."

"Larry?"

"No. Um, here's what happened," he began, his voice barely above a whisper. Joyce leaned in closer, struggling to understand. "There was a tap on my window. When I pulled back the blinds, it was a woman I've seen around here before, but I don't know her name, and she *hissed* me."

"She hissed?"

He shook his head, as if hissing were a silly notion. "No, no, she didn't hiss at me. She HEXED me."

"Come again?"

"I know it sounds crazy." *Yep.* "But I've had diarrhea ever since, and now I've got this weird rash on my—"

"Don't need specifics."

"Right. The thing is… I've got a really hot date, and I can't spend the whole night on the can. And what if we go back to her place?" Andy dropped his head into his hands, digging his fingers through his hair. "I look like I have herpes!"

Joyce pressed her hand against her forehead. "Is it possible there is no hex and you actually have herpes?"

"No way, man. I only dig clean."

What?

The door swung open and in charged Daniella in an itsy bitsy yellow bikini. "Yoyce," she snapped, propping her hands on her hips, just above the strings holding her bottoms up. "I have a problem."

Andy backed away, shielding his hexed manhood with both hands. Joyce followed his terrified gaze. "Daniella, did you do something to Andy?"

"Yes, I hexed him," she replied, not skipping a beat.

Andy's face contorted into a *told you so!* look, his hands still cupping his crotch. The back door opened, and Robin from Apartment 19 slid in. She joined the group robed in a muumuu-looking dress you'd expect to see on a *Golden Girl*. "Hey Joyce, what's my September rent?"

"Same as last month," replied Joyce.

"But there are only thirty days in September?"

Daniella nodded. "We should prorate the month of September. I won't pay for one more day."

"Dude, what about the hex?" pleaded Andy, now cowering behind the curtain.

Joyce pinched the bridge of her nose. "Daniella, unhex Andy so he can go digging tonight."

Daniella crossed her arms over her chest, pointing her nose up as if someone had just farted. "I won't lift the hex. I don't like him. He parks too close to my car in the carport. It makes it hard for me to get out."

I need a smoke. "Andy, you be more careful when you park, and Daniella, you lift the hex."

Andy was quick to oblige, while Daniella reluctantly murmured, "Fine."

Robin raised her hand, and a stack of golden bangles slid down her arm. "Um, excuse me? So you're saying I should prorate September?"

"No, Robin. Daniella, hex."

Daniella rolled her eyes and then spit into her palm, slapped her hands together and snapped her fingers. "There, it's lifted. I'm going swimming now. Wait, you know there is a mattress in there? That's why I came in."

Right. Mattress. Slipped my mind.

"The rash is still there!" cried Andy, taking a gander down his pants.

"That's because I have no hexing abilities, moron," Daniella cackled.

"Eww, TMI," Robin said.

Joyce stared at the ceiling. *Damn you, California tobacco regulations.* "Robin, rent is the same every month no matter how many days. We had this conversation in February and in April. Now, I've got to go deal with the mattress."

"What? That's ridiculous!" She threw her hands up so fast a bangle went sailing across the room and landed on the coffee table.

"What about my rash?"

"See a doctor," Joyce offered over her shoulder as she shuffled into her apartment and closed the door. She quickly lit a cigarette and closed her eyes as the nicotine fed the all-consuming craving, soothing the anxiety and calming the hand tremors. Through the warped wood she could still hear Andy complaining about his red wiener.

I'm getting too old for this.

Two more long drags, and broaching the mattress situation felt feasible.

Bob was in his recliner, sleeping, as usual. He used to walk the property all day, fixing things that didn't need fixing. Chatting with residents. Organizing the maintenance garage. Now he spent his time watching court shows—*People's Court, Judge Judy, Judge Mathis, Judge Joe Brown, Paternity Court, Divorce Court.* If a hotheaded judge was involved, he watched it. She took up smoking. He took up daytime court television. Everyone copes with grief differently.

Judge Longwood from *The Friendship Court* banged her gavel, startling Bob awake before Joyce had the chance. With a low grumble, he reached down and pulled the handle on the side of the recliner. The footrest jumped into place, and he pushed back and readjusted, scratching at the gray whiskers scattered across his chin, settling in for his fifth catnap of the day. Despite his scruff, and the fact he'd been sporting the same outfit since Monday—jeans, shirt with *Maintenance* embroidered above the breast pocket, and his almost sole-less New Balance shoes—he was still as handsome as ever. Piercing blue eyes, a thick head of dark gray hair (once brown), with a dimple in the middle of his chin.

Joyce stood over her husband, debating whether to wake him or let him be. Before the accident, there'd be no hesitation. She'd lean down and plant a kiss on his forehead. He'd wake up, flash a sheepish grin and run his hands down his clean-shaven face, or he'd pull her down and wrap his muscular arms around her, refusing to let go. She'd fuss and tell him to "get your butt to work" and then he'd say "yes, ma'am" or "yes, captain" and slap her tush. They'd been sweethearts since grade school. Now, they were practically strangers.

Joyce tapped Bob on the shoulder. He didn't budge. She tapped him again. This time he stirred and swiped at her hand. "What's wrong?" he groaned, his eyes still clamped shut.

"There's a mattress in the pool. I tried to get it out, but it's too heavy," she whispered, not exactly sure why she was.

Bob moaned and grumbled, then reached down for the handle of the recliner and sprung upright. "I'll take care of it," he told the television and left out the front door. No "yes ma'am," no spanking, not even a glance in her direction.

Five letter word for unitary... alone.

Chapter 5

Cambria

"Hello?"

"Hello, how are you doing?" I answered with a big smile.

"Who is this?"

Right. "My name is Cambria. I'm calling regarding the nanny position you posted on Craigslist. Is it still available?"

"Do you have previous nanny experience?"

Technically no, but, "I have a three-year old daughter."

"So that would be a no?"

Damn. "Correct, but I love children, and I'm very good with them." Especially for twenty-four dollars an hour—five dollars more than I made at Bart's. Who knew babysitting was where the money was?

"Where did you graduate from?"

"Fresno."

"State?"

"High school." *If parenting doesn't require a degree, why would babysitting?* "Did I mention I'm very good with children?"

Long pause. "I'm sorry, but we're looking for at least a Bachelor's in Early Childhood Development and/or ten years' experience and fluent in at least two languages. But thank you for calling."

Click.

Crap. *Mierda.* See? I could speak two languages.

Chapter 6

Joyce

Life changed on a Tuesday. The sun was high in the crystal sky, casing the community in beautiful rays of spring sunlight. California water restrictions had stripped the landscape of flowers, yet on this day, the spiky drought-resistant plants had transformed from a dowdy brown to vibrant hues of green and purple, adding joyful pops of color. The air tasted of chlorine and SPF. Children with goggles wrapped tightly around their eyes tiptoed on the pool deck, careful not to burn their feet on the scorching surface.

Bob offered to man the office so Joyce could enjoy the first day of spring, her favorite season, outside surrounded by her residents. She parked herself at the picnic table by the pool with the latest John Grisham in hand, appreciating the warmth on her skin and the shrieks of laughter from the children as they cannonballed into the deep end.

Then, it happened.

One moment Joyce's brown eyes were soaking in the words of her favorite author, and a single blink later they were watching Silvia Kravitz running through the breezeway. Joyce closed the book, being sure to dog-ear her page, and folded her hands, waiting. Silvia treated every maintenance request as if it were a life-threatening emergency. Clogged toilets, jammed quarter slot, massive flood—they all received the same over-the-top reaction.

This time felt different though. It wasn't because of the urgency in Silvia's steps, and it wasn't because of the emotion on her face (she had none—the woman was eighty percent Botox, and the rest was silicone). Dread swirled around in Joyce's stomach as if she had just eaten five-day-old Chinese takeout.

Before Silvia could get the words "Something's happened!" out of her mouth, Joyce was up and running, going as fast as her mature limbs would take her.

A sheriff stood at her front door in his pressed tan shirt, black tie and creased pants. Joyce came to a halt, the adrenalin pumping so fast she feared she may pass out, but one glance at the floor told her Bob beat her to it.

Josh.

There was no reason to think it. Josh had never been in trouble with the law. He wasn't sick. He kept to his routine. At work by seven, lunch at noon, home by six. He called her at eight, in bed by eleven.

She begged the officer with her eyes not to say it, not to confirm what she knew in her heart had already happened.

But he didn't listen.

With a sorrowful expression and a soft voice, the sheriff said, "I'm so sorry. Your son was involved in a car accident, and first responders did everything they could…"

This was the day Bob retreated to his recliner, and Joyce stopped giving a damn.

PART TWO

Chapter 7

Cambria

If hiking uphill while wearing a Ninja Turtle costume doesn't have you questioning every life choice you've ever made, then I don't know what will.

The customer requested I not park near the home, so as to not offend partygoers with my "unsightly" Civic, and that I dress in the car, so as not to offend the bathroom with my Target clothing.

"Whatever you wish," I responded, eager to please. The Beverly Hills birthday bash for Razor and thirty of his closest friends carried promise of a big tip.

Rent was counting on it.

My car provided limited changing space. Lilly's mammoth of a car seat took up most of the backseat, making my Michelangelo transformation difficult. *"When slipping on the costume, you say goodbye to Cambria and hello to Michelangelo, a fun-loving, pizza-eating nunchuck-swinging turtle. Got it?"* Deb, from The People Perfect Party Palace Place explained during my twenty-minute training session.

I nodded, took Michelangelo, left my dignity, and proceeded to the party. Problem was, the bulky polyester fabric was uncooperative. So were the clown-like green shoes, shell and ten-pound smiling turtle head. There was no "slipping" into anything. Except out the car door when finished, as if my Civic just birthed a mutant. I landed on my back, partially on the sidewalk, mostly in the gutter with my oversized green foot tangled in the seatbelt.

It's said a turtle will die if flipped onto its shell. I concede. A small piece of me croaked right there.

I engaged in an awkward combination of rocking and thrusting and kicking and swearing before a police officer pulled over and propped me upright. After I passed the sobriety test, I made the uphill trek in the 100-degree heat, swathed in polyester, chanting *rent, rent, rent, rent* to keep from crying. Physical activity is not a strength of mine.

The gate securing Razor's McMansion was a lovely, intricate design of wrought iron with swirls and scrolls and a "W" in the middle... or... actually... an "M." It was only a "W" from my upside-down position, draped over the call box, puffing air through the mesh peephole of the turtle head.

Note to self: You're broke. Suck it up.

Once she granted me entrance through the gate, Razor's mother met me at the front door, leaning against the jamb with a mimosa in her diamond-encrusted hand. She had on a floor-length sheer turquoise dress. Her platinum hair and makeup looked professionally done, and her teeny wrists were wrapped in diamonds, and her neck draped in gold, like she had put on every piece of jewelry she owned for the occasion.

"They're out back," she told me, stepping away, as to not accidently come in contact with Michelangelo. Not that I blamed her. Inside, the costume reeked like vomit and sweat with a hint of Febreze. I assumed the outside didn't smell much better.

The Mother led me into a vast entryway, through a kitchen filled with shiny appliances, marble counters, and a round island big enough to double as King Arthur's table. Even through a Ninja Turtle's teeth (where my mesh peephole was located) the house looked lavish and immaculate. The creamy drapes appeared to waterfall from the ceiling, and the dining room chandelier was the size of my car. The walls looked as if they were constructed of gold and imprinted with vines and flowers and women with bare backs down to the top of their butt cracks. *Must be a rich people thing.*

The backyard was mostly pool. The Mother instructed me to wait at the back door while she gathered the children, and I stood as ordered. Hot. Nervous. Mortified. Performing in front of a crowd went against every natural instinct I had. Memories of my sixth grade piano recital filled my head. I had barfed all over the keys during a slow rendition of *Alouette*.

"Here children! Here, here!" the Mother shouted, as if calling for the dog. "Look who it is."

That's my cue.

I strutted out and stood before a group of kids garbed in Ninja Turtle apparel, with painted green faces and plastic shells secured to their backs. I waved and wiggled my shoulders and shot my thumbs up in the air, as instructed by Deb. And they loved it. The children were star-struck. The look of enchantment beaming from their little green faces was invigorating. It was as if I were a Hemsworth brother or something.

"OK, gather around, and let's take pictures," The Mother said, and just like that, armies of adults armed with iPhones appeared out of nowhere.

One thing I had learned during my employment famine was that I sweat, profusely, when nervous. My vision began clouding from the salty liquid dribbling down my face.

Oh, the nunchucks.

Deb told me to take them out when I posed for pictures. I reached down and grabbed the plastic weapon from the belt wrapped around my turtle waist and... *crap!* I whacked a child across the face. Of course, he started to cry.

I bent down in an attempt to comfort the little boy I just belted. *"Be sure not to bend down too fast,"* Deb had warned—and for good reason. The Michelangelo head went all exorcist and flipped around, turning my world black and eliciting cries from another four or five children.

Crap! I stood up quickly, too quickly. I felt sick.

"Remember to breathe," Deb had said. *"You don't want to pass out."*

Heeding her advice, I took rapid breaths while struggling with my giant hands to spin the head around. Finally, the turtle head twirled on right. I was able to see again. Mostly black dots and mostly scared little faces and mostly the... ground...

Chapter 8

Joyce

When Joyce saw Kevin approaching the office, all she heard was the Jaws theme song. *Duunnn dunnn... duunnnn dunnn... duunnnnnn... dun.*

There was an unspoken territory agreement between them. The third courtyard was his terrain, the first courtyard hers, and the pool neutral. It was easier this way. When Kevin did breach the buffer, it was never for the intent of pleasantries. He was angry. Last time, he was furious Bob had painted the newly installed laundry room door. "The wood needs to breathe, live and procreate. You can't paint over it. It'll die."

Joyce broke the news that the particleboard was already dead and, therefore, incapable of breeding. This pissed him off. Eventually, Bob was able to calm him down. He was good at that.

Unfortunately, Bob had given up on life. The recliner had become his deathbed and the television his life-support system and Judge Judy his caretaker. Only his bladder and the occasional maintenance emergency could summon him from his spot. He would be of no help in this case, which was a shame, because for the first time in twenty-five years, Joyce knew exactly why Kevin was storming toward the office all clenched fists and red-faced—he was, of course, angry. But for first time in twenty-five years, he had good reason to be.

Dun dun dun dun dun...

Chapter 9

Cambria

I forced an eyelid half open and saw a sapphire sky filled with flying babies. Each towhead infant was armed with a bow and arrow, with poorly swathed diapers exposing their butts. *Where the hell am I?*

Then it hit me.

A Nerf dart to the face.

"Told you it was dead," I heard a little boy whisper in the distance. "Watch, I'll shoot it again."

Ouch! I placed my hand on my aching head, feeling the itchy fabric on my face. *What the... why am I wearing gloves?*

"It's moving!" A throng of ear-piercing shrieks broke out, slicing through my skull like a machete. "Zombie! Zombie!"

The pattering of little-soled shoes jolted my oblongata awake. Everything came flooding back like in a bad dream. The party. The parents. The kids. The nunchucks. The ground.

"Oh, no. Please, no," I moaned, attempting to roll to my side, finding myself in the same precarious shell-down position as earlier—stuck. Crap.

Forcing both eyes open, I took surveillance of my surroundings. Somehow, I had been moved to a room with a mural of battling babies painted on the ceiling. *Must be a rich person thing.*

"Never mind, she's awake," I heard The Mother say. Heels clanked on the marble flooring until she appeared over me with a refilled mimosa in hand. "I called off the ambulance," she said.

Good thing, because I no longer had insurance.

"Can you stand up?" she asked, extending an arm that sparkled with jewels.

I nodded, slipping my three-fingered mutant hand into her dainty grasp. She heaved with all her little might until I managed a standing position. I felt queasy and embarrassed and green. Very green.

"OK, let's go," The Mother said, dumping Michelangelo back on my head. "You have no idea how embarrassing that was for me."

Oh, I think I do.

She hurried me to the front door, past the fancy this and fancy that, determined to get me out as soon as possible. I struggled to keep up, forcing my webbed feet to move as fast as she was.

Out the front door we went. "Hold on a second. I have something for you," The Mother said before releasing me into the wild. I waited while she disappeared from my meshy line of sight.

"Afterward, you're responsible for collecting payment. You'll then return the check to me along with the costume, and only then will you get paid. Sometimes they tip. Be sure to act surprised and gracious if they do," Deb had instructed. Acting surprised wouldn't be difficult. My hope for a tip disappeared when I hit the ground. At least I'd get paid, and that should cover rent—if I stopped eating.

The Mother returned with a bottle of water. "Drink

this once you feel better so you don't vomit on the driveway."

"Wait, I'm supposed to get a check for The Perfect..." I was too woozy to finish the mouthful of a name.

"No, no. They called in a professional turtle. It should be here soon. You can go." Before she closed the door, she paused to give me this helpful tidbit of advice: "I would find a different occupation if I were you."

Gee.

Thanks.

I walked down the driveway with my giant turtle head hung low. The neighboring mansion was undergoing a remodel, and a Dumpster sat at the curb, providing much needed shade. I leaned against the bin, slid down to my butt, and removed the suffocating turtle head.

Ugh.

My last unemployment check had been cashed and spent. My credit had taken a swift nosedive into the red. I had no more money. I wouldn't be able to cover rent on the first. I'd held out for a job I felt worthy of my skills— but one never came. Nearly six months. Stupid pride. Now I was going to have to take two measly paying jobs to cover my expenses and go bald in the process.

Please, please, let this be rock bottom.

There was a click and a squeak and shriek and... there went the Dumpster. Rolling down the hill.

"Oh, no, no, no, no!" I yanked the gloves off with my teeth and grabbed the side, using my heels as brakes, because apparently I believed I had Superman-like powers.

Note to self: You don't.

The Dumpster slipped out of my grasp and went barreling down the hill, gaining more and more momentum as it went. I ran after it, wobbling as fast as my webbed feet would allow.

First went the Dumpster.

Then came the Ninja Turtle.

How this didn't get captured on video and go viral was beyond me.

"Stop!" I yelled, as if the hunk of metal and wood hurtling into oncoming traffic had ears.

To my surprise, the Dumpster obeyed my command. Stopping at the end of the street before cruising onto the main road. Unfortunately, a car thwarted its journey.

The car: mine.

Right into the driver's side door.

"Why?" I cried, falling to my knees, feeling very much like a failure in a half shell...

Loser power!

Chapter 10

Joyce

Dun dun dun dun dun dun...

Kevin entered the lobby, chest first (the chest in question unclothed and hairy). He wore dark mid-thigh corduroy shorts and mismatched tube socks with a roll of masking tape as a bracelet. He gave the floral armchair a look of disgust as he passed.

"What's going on, Kevin?" Joyce asked, trying to sound casual.

Kevin placed a stack of papers, roll of tape and elbows on the counter. "This place is ugly," he said, as he usually did. He'd never been a fan of the lobby décor; said it was outdated, and Joyce should have gone with a cabana theme. "That's not why I'm here though. I want to hang these reward flyers in the office."

"Reward?"

"I'm offering twenty bucks for information on who had me arrested last night."

Joyce took a breath. *Damn.*

The emergency line had rung multiple times the night before, all Kevin complaints.

At 1:00 a.m., he was playing his music too loudly.

Joyce called his cell, and he promised to turn it down.

At 3:00 a.m., he was on his patio singing along with the music.

Joyce called his cell, and he didn't answer.

It was at 4:00 a.m., when Kevin took his performance to the community picnic table and added in choreography, sans clothes, that Joyce snapped. All the years of dealing with Kevin, the months of being ignored by Bob, and the unbearable misery of Josh's death came to a head and erupted out of her like fiery lava.

All she saw was red.

Joyce groped for the phone on her nightstand, intending to leave a strongly worded voicemail for Kevin.

Except she didn't.

Her finger dialed 9-1-1 robotically. She reported a "disturbance" in the third courtyard and gave no further information. She didn't feel an ounce of guilt about it either. Until now.

Joyce genuinely believed the police would just talk to Kevin about respecting his neighbors and, if anything, he'd be scared into submission. His being arrested never crossed her mind.

"What were the charges?" she asked.

"I was charged with two counts of none-of-your-business. I'm so pissed off!" He pounded the counter with his fist.

Joyce jumped.

"I will find out who it was, Joyce. I will."

This is bad.

When Kevin put his mind to something, he thought and spoke of nothing else. Lucky for him, he didn't have any adult responsibilities to interfere.

"You know who I think it was?" Kevin asked, drumming his fingers along his jawline. "I think it was the lady next door, the one with the kid. I can't stand parents. Especially mothers. They think because they have a baby suddenly everyone needs to cater to them. *Oh, my baby's asleep. Be quiet. Oh, don't smoke around my baby. Oh, don't walk around naked in front of my baby.* I'm not the one who forced her to push out a kid, why should I be punished? I want her gone, today. Let's make that happen. Give me the notice, and I'll deliver it. Her kid can go cry on the streets for all I care."

Joyce rubbed her temples. "I don't think it was her. She's never complained before." *A miracle.*

"Let's get the paperwork started," he said, ignoring her. "You've been slipping, and there's no excuse for it. You've let some serious deadbeats in here. Let's start cleaning this place up. Starting with my neighbor."

It happened again. The red. "Shut your mouth you entitled imbecile! I'm the one who called, not any of your neighbors!"

Silence. And then Kevin's face contorted into an all-consuming anger. He looked around the room until his eyes landed on the crystal vase of flowers on the counter.

Red gone.

"Kevin, don't. That was a Mother's Day present from Josh."

He picked up the vase and held it high in the air with an *I'll show you* smirk.

"Put it down, carefully, please," Joyce pleaded. "I kept getting calls. I told them your family owned the building, and I explained your situation. But people can only take so much. You've got to know this."

He shook his head. "There is no *situation*, and you know this, Joyce."

"I know." If he weren't holding her last Mother's Day present hostage, then she may have felt sorry for Kevin. As she usually did. His *situation* or lack thereof, was terrible. But as it stood, nothing but anger was pumping through her veins. *So help me, if he breaks my vase...* "Put it down!"

Kevin's eyed darted around the room again, his head shaking, his chest rising and falling as if he'd just performed jumping jacks.

He looked at the counter.

Then at her.

Then at the counter.

Then at the floral armchair.

Without a word, he turned and darted out the door, taking the vase with him.

No!

Joyce followed, shuffling as fast as she could, coughing and wheezing the entire journey. Pushing her lungs past their natural capacity. Kevin's apartment bridged over the back walkway, at the top of the stairwell. It was the only door painted black.

Joyce knocked. "Vase... please... give it... back," she gasped, forcing the words.

For once Kevin listened—in his own "Kevin" kind of way.

The vase crashed through the window and into the railing, shattering into thousands of tiny pieces. Joyce pressed her back against the wall, not able to cry, not able to make any noise. She could only stare at the glass shards spewed across the walkway, unable to decipher which belonged to the window and which belonged to her heart.

She clutched the railing, and eased herself down the stairs. She collapsed on the bottom step and dropped her face into her hands.

Josh.

Someone brushed against her arm as they zoomed by. "You've seen your last day, Kevin! You hear me?"

Bob?

Joyce looked up. Bob stood at the top of the stairwell, looking haggard and grubby with his fist beating on the black door. Kevin didn't answer.

"You come near my wife again, and I'll take you down!"

Joyce's mouth dropped. She'd never heard Bob threaten anyone before. *Must be all that court television.*

Seething, Bob charged down the stairs and paced the walkway in front of Joyce, going back and forth, back and forth, back and forth. Mumbling indecipherable words. Wringing his hands. Pacing a mile's worth of steps before he finally stopped.

He stood in front of Joyce, exhaled a deep breath, and extended a helping arm. She hesitated, then slowly wrapped her fingers around his bicep and stood. He pulled her into an embrace, placing his hand on the back of her head. His lips close to her ear. "I've got you, sweetie," he whispered.

Sweetie.

With that, tears sprung to her eyes. Tears for her vase. Tears from Bob's whiskers prickling her face. Tears for the endearing term she hadn't heard in months. Tears for the familiar warmth of being tucked into the arms of the man she'd loved since she was twelve years old.

"Shh, I've got you," he repeated.

Chapter 11

Cambria

With sand in my shoes and the sun on my back, I stretched my arms high above my head and gave Lilly a big push on the swing, sending her to "the moon."

"Higher!" she begged, and I obliged (after a requested "puh-lease" was delivered).

"There's my girl," Tom greeted, walking through the overgrown park grass, his tall shadow arriving before him. He had on his business attire—suit, white shirt, tie, leather messenger bag crossed over his chest, and his dark hair gelled to the side.

"Stop me. Stop me. Stop me," Lilly demanded, kicking her feet in panic. I did as told (after a "puh-lease") and grabbed the old chains of the swing, slowing her to a speed she deemed suitable to hurl herself off, not able to wait any longer. She raced over to her daddy. Tom picked her up and threw her high in the air. Too high. I watched with one eye shut.

"You ready to spend the weekend with Daddy?" he asked, brushing a curl out of her eyes.

"Yes!" she replied, squishing Tom's cheeks between

her hands. "I can go so high on the swing. All by myself. Wanna see? Wanna see? Wanna see? Wanna see?"

"*No way,*" Tom said with exaggerated disbelief.

"I can. All by myself. No help. Watch." With a cheerful shriek, Lilly twisted out of Tom's arms and raced to the swing. She climbed on the seat and instructed *me* to push her to the moon so *she* could do it all by *herself*. If only such illogical statements were as cute in adults as they were in toddlers, I'd have many more suitors than the zero I currently had.

"Why are we meeting at the park instead of your apartment?" Tom asked from the ledge of the sandbox.

"Fresh air." *And my landlord is in the office from nine to three on Fridays, and I don't have rent, so I'm avoiding going home until he's gone.*

I'd be forced to tell Tom about my financial ruin eventually. Hopefully I'd find the nerve before I took up residence on the park bench he was currently standing in front of.

"How's the job hunt going?"

"It's... *going.* I have a *gig* I'll be starting in five to seven days. Speaking of which, didn't you represent someone who owned a wig shop?"

He thought, then shook his head. "Why?"

"No reason."

"I have something for you." Tom flipped open his bag and pulled out a newspaper. "I'm done reading this if you want it."

"For what?" I wasn't officially homeless. Yet.

"For the classifieds. Here, take it."

I took the paper and looked it over, my other hand still pushing Lilly.

Huh, do people still advertise in print only?

time she drove past, she felt like yelling, *No duh, Sherlock* (or however the saying went). *Why do you think I'm smoking more?*

She used the door in lieu of an ashtray, stubbing out her cigarette, already aching for another. *Let's make this quick.* "What are you doing, Daniella?" she asked in her raspy voice. She'd been hoarse most of her life, a botched tonsillectomy in the fifties.

"Yoyce, I'm doing nothing," replied Daniella in her thick accent.

Carmen's eyes nearly exploded out of her head. "She won't plug the machines back in so I can do my laundry!"

"I told her I was using the laundry room right now. When I'm done, she can have it. Whether I do my laundry or whether I do my cooking, what's the difference? I pay my rent. I can use my laundry room how I want," Daniella said with a patronizing smirk.

"This is not your laundry room!" Carmen screamed.

Seven started crying.

The kitchen timer dinged.

Lexie from Apartment 3 walked in with her phone sandwiched between her shoulder and ear. She stepped over Carmen's laundry basket and yanked open the dryer. "What the hell? Why are my clothes damp?" She turned around. Her eyes darted around the room from the crockpot, to the screaming women, then to Joyce. "The dryer isn't plugged in!" She took in a big breath, ready to spew her mind, but before she could, Joyce interjected.

"Settle down, settle down, ladies. I've got—" But she launched into a coughing fit before she could finish. Her eighty-pound frame quaked violently with each blast of expelled air.

There was no mistaking, this was a result of the nicotine.

"Hold on, my apartment manager is, like, dying," Lexie said to her phone, and poked Joyce's shoulder with

Chapter 12

Joyce

The kettle whistled. Bob grabbed two mugs from the cabinet and poured them both a cup of chamomile. Joyce stubbed out her cigarette in the ashtray still smoldering from her last deposit and used the dissolving wad of Kleenex in her hand to dab her eyes. She hadn't felt so emotionally drained since the funeral.

Bob placed their tea on the table and slid into the chair next to hers.

"I'm so mad I could scream," she said, placing another cigarette between her lips. "Or sue. I should sue him for the cost of my vase. That's what I should do. I'm sure it cost Josh a pretty quarter or two."

Bob reached over and took the cigarette out of her mouth, then placed it between them. He studied it for some time before standing. Joyce sunk. He would now retreat back to his television. It was nearly time for *Divorce Court.*

She slid the cigarette back between her lips just as Bob returned with a copy of *The Yellow Pages.*

"What are you doing?" she asked, both surprised and

relieved.

"Why shouldn't you sue for your vase and emotional damage too?" He opened the thick book, licked his finger and flipped through the pages.

"You're not trying to get us on one of your shows, are you?"

"I'd love to see Judge Jubilee from *Jubilee Justice* really hand it to him, but we'd have more success with an attorney," he said, running his finger down the list of law firms.

"But, Bob, Kevin doesn't have any money."

He reached for the phone. "His parents do. We're forced to leave because of the hostile environment *they've* created." He started dialing. "We'll sue for the salary of five years, when we would retire, and we'll buy a place in Nevada. We always said we wanted to live there."

"I don't know, Bob. I don't want Elder Management to get in trouble. Not after everything they've done for us." Her boss, Patrick, had taken great care of them— bonuses, vacations, several raises, funeral costs. It's the only reason they'd put up with Kevin for as long as they had.

"We won't, we'll go after the McMills family directly," Bob said with conviction.

"I don't know..."

He reached over and grabbed her hand, giving it a reassuring squeeze, just as he used to before Judge Judy got involved. "I'm done not living. This isn't what *he* would want. I can't stand to look at this place any more. The walls. The front door. It's got too many reminders of the day... I don't want to remember the day he died. I want to remember all the days before. This is our ticket to get out of this purgatory. Let's take it." He lifted the collar of his shirt to wipe the tears spilling down his cheeks.

She closed her eyes, preparing for her own tears. She

felt the same. Josh had never lived in their apartment. He had already started college by the time she took the job. Every time she stepped foot out their front door, she thought of the sheriff standing in his creased pants and tan shirt telling her Josh had died. "I want to. I really do. But who is Patrick going to get to replace me? No experienced property manager will put up with Kevin like we have."

He placed the phone to his ear. "Sweetie, that is not your problem... Hello, yes, I would like to speak with an attorney regarding a hostile work environment."

Chapter 13

Cambria

Nearly three o'clock. I'd already witnessed one person peeing in the duck pond, two teenagers making out behind the slide and three drug deals. It was time to go home.

I gathered my belongings: sack lunch, criminal thrillers borrowed from the library, water bottle, and Tom's copy of the newspaper (which I had been using as a barrier between the mysterious goo on the park bench and my butt). I held the paper, eyeing the nearby trashcan. Seemed odd there would be a job listed in print that wasn't on the sites I scoured daily. Did anyone even read the newspaper any more? Aside from Tom?

It was worth a look. I unfolded the paper, flipped to the classified section, and glanced over the listings. As suspected, all looked familiar. I'd either applied and hadn't heard back, applied and didn't get the job, or the qualifications were well out of my realm (not that it stopped me from applying anyhow. Never know.) Near the bottom of the page, however, in bold lettering was one ad I hadn't seen before. It was either new or had been lost in the filter or perhaps it really was only in print.

> Seeking an on-site Apartment Property Manager for a charming 40-unit community. Applicant must have excellent organizational skills and a calming demeanor. Strong problem solving skills are a must. Applicant must be dependable, punctual and able to multitask without becoming easily frazzled. Starting at 30K + bonus + benefits + two-bedroom apartment + utilities. Experience a plus.

This can't be right. With salary and housing, the annual income would average close to 60K, not counting bonuses. This was higher than the nanny jobs listed. *For forty units? That's it?* The ad was oddly specific on personality qualifications, with emphasis on "must," but without mention of software or education requirements. Seemed almost too good to be true. Yes, I didn't have any property management experience. But I lived in an apartment, and I had been a manager. Apartment + Manager = Apartment Manager. *Voilà.*

I grabbed my cell and dialed the number listed.

"Elder Property Management," a woman answered.

"Hello, I'm calling about the manager position at the charming forty-unit community. Is it still available?"

"It is. Would you like the fax number?"

Sweet! "I would, thank you. Real quick question first. I wanted to verify—the salary is thirty thousand a year, and the apartment and utilities do or do not come out of that amount?"

"Do not. The apartment and utilities are additional compensation."

Wow. Seemed high for a relatively easy job. Granted, my own apartment manager was probably banging on my door while I was hiding in the park. So, worst case, I would have a tenant like me.

"Can I get that fax number, please?" I asked, fishing a pen and scrap of paper out of my bag.

Chapter 14

Joyce

Joyce took a sip of grape juice. The Internet said this would help her quit smoking by releasing toxins, or something like that. She was off to the loo every twenty minutes and still ached for a cigarette. But she and Bob made a promise. She'd quit smoking, and he'd quit television. She was down to two packs a day and eight glasses of juice, while Bob was down to six hours of television, and he returned to their bed at night instead of sleeping in his recliner. Progress.

She placed the juice on the desk and wiggled the computer mouse, waking up the monitor. Displayed on the screen was 1,600 square feet of prefabricated perfection. Their new home—a white clapboard single-story with blue shutters, wraparound porch and, most importantly, not a single shared wall with any neighbor. It felt good to have something to look forward to. Almost... exciting.

The pain of losing Josh would never go away, but at least she had Bob by her side again. Having him there brought a hint of warmth back to her life. She felt assured they'd now be able to enjoy the time they had left, until the blessed day she would meet Josh in "paradise" as Joyce called it.

It didn't even require a lawyer. Kevin's family was quick to throw money at them to keep their mouths shut. It was a darn shame for Kevin. Not so much for Joyce and Bob.

Still, her loyalty was to Patrick, and after twenty-five years, it seemed the least she could do was stay long enough to train her replacement.

The door chimed and in came Chase, the new maintenance man Patrick had hired. According to Bob, he wasn't particularly skilled. He sure was a nice piece of eye sugar (or however that saying went) for the residents though.

"Do you have any work orders?" Chase asked, running a hand through his blond mane.

"Do I have work orders?" she repeated. *Ha!* She placed all seventeen orders on the counter. "You can start with these."

There had been a notable increase in maintenance requests. Silly things. Lexie's garbage disposal now clogged daily. Trisha's wall "makes an odd buzzing sound" but only when she's alone. Chase had logged far too many hours trying to locate the noise.

"Do you know if he's single?" Carmen had asked when she called earlier to complain about her garbage disposal. "Don't ask him. I was just curious. For a friend," she quickly added.

"I'm sure I don't know the answer to that question," Joyce told her, and offered to send Bob to take a look at her disposal instead, when, miraculously, Carmen was able to fix it herself. By plugging it in.

The guy was good-looking, she'd give them that, but his messy hair and five o'clock shadow (no matter the time) weren't her style. His eyes were lovely though. An emerald green. And he was a good kid, very charming. But she liked a clean-shaved man—like Bob.

"These should keep me busy for a while," Chase said, flipping through the stack of work orders.

"Good, get to work then," Joyce said, shooing him out of the lobby. "I'm expecting an applicant here any second, and Patrick is running late."

"I'm surprised you haven't found someone yet. Aren't you guys leaving soon?"

"Yep, cutting it close. Crossing my toes for this one." The fact it was ten minutes before the scheduled interview and she had yet to arrive wasn't promising though. "Oh, Chase, before I forget. Carmen wants to know if you're single." *Or was I not supposed to ask that?*

"Um... I am but—"

"Oh, dear." Joyce shook her head. "This is no good. We'll tell everyone you're not. When it comes to residents, mark my words: Be friendly with everyone. Make friends with no one. Never mix business and pleasure. Especially in this business."

"Thanks. I'll... keep that in mind." He smiled and grabbed his work orders, examining the pile as he walked out.

Joyce returned to her desk and checked the time— almost noon. *Applicant must be dependable, punctual...* the ad said. Important qualities her replacement *must* possess. Which is why Joyce wrote the ad herself.

The door chimed. In came Wysteria, the girlfriend of Vincent in Apartment 39. She'd been around a lot lately. Too much. Joyce knew she was living there, and moving in without filling out an application and being approved is a major no-no.

"Application," Joyce reminded Wysteria. "Bring it in."

She removed the Tootsie Pop from her mouth. "Totally on it," she said with a wink.

Joyce grunted and rolled her eyes. Experience told her it would take at least five more reminders before the application showed up on her desk. *That can be the new manager's problem.*

She was admiring the picture of her new home when the door chimed again. This time, in came a girl. A young thing with a freckled face, a mass of dark curly hair, blue eyes, a stain on the front of her dress and scrapes on her knees. "Hi. Are you Joyce?" the girl asked.

"I am."

She looked disappointed. "I'm Cambria Clyne. I have an interview with Patrick for the apartment management position. His secretary told me to meet him here at noon."

The girl, Cambria, was a sweaty mess. If an interview made her flustered, then she'd never survive as an on-site manager. Which prompted Joyce to ask, "Hmm, *you* really want *this* job?" *Kevin will eat her alive.*

"Yes, I do," Cambria replied.

Joyce regarded her. She was a cute girl. They already had a cute maintenance man.

Oh, what the hell?

Epilogue

Joyce

Joyce told Patrick she'd stay till Friday. She didn't, however, say what time on Friday. And if there's one thing Joyce hated, it was prolonging the inevitable. Nine in the morning seemed like a nice time to get out of there.

After a quick goodbye to the new manager, Bob slammed on the gas, and they were gone. Joyce watched the property she had spent the last twenty-five years of her life managing disappear in the rearview mirror. She exhaled, feeling the weight leave her shoulders.

"Next stop, Nevada!" Bob said, merging onto the freeway. "No more emergency calls. No more work orders. No more Kevin. We're free. Ready for the slots?" He turned to Joyce, who flashed him a mischievous smile. "What's that smile for?"

"I did something."

His smile dropped. "What did you do?"

She turned around and pointed to the box in the backseat. "I copied all of Kevin's files and brought them with me."

"Why would you *ever* want to do that?"

"The Man-Child Chronicles," she said, as if it were obvious.

"No, sweetie. No, no. Put it behind you. You'll get sued. We'll get sued. Let's wash our hands of that family."

Joyce shrugged. "Who cares if they sue? We'll be long gone before they collect a nickel. I'll publish it anonymously. You told me when you retired from teaching you would write a book. Well, here's your chance. Help me write this one."

Bob shook his head, staring at the road ahead.

It wasn't until they reached the border that he turned to her and said, "Sure, what the hell?"

A Note from Erin Huss

Hello!

I want to personally thank you. Yes, YOU, the one with the book/phone/Kindle/tablet in your hand. You're awesome, and don't let anyone tell you otherwise. It took six years of on-site property management and lots of writing (and candy) to get here, and I appreciate you taking the time out of your busy life to read *For Hire*.

If you enjoyed the book, it would make my day if you left a review on Amazon. The more reviews I get, the more books I can sell, the more sales I have, the more See's Candy I can buy, the more See's I eat, the more energy I have to write. And don't you want to know what happens next?

I'd also like to invite you to join my mailing list to stay up to date on my latest news and special sales, and get a free ebook of *Can't Pay My Rent* (normally $2.99)! You can sign up here: http://bit.ly/erinhussnews

My sincerest thanks,
Erin

P.S. Read on for a sneak peek of *For Rent*, a romantic comedy about Cambria's struggles as an apartment manager.

Acknowledgements

I want to thank Adria Cimino and Vicki Lesage for the opportunity to write *For Hire*; George at the Shell station for the information on what brand of cigarettes Joyce might smoke, and for always asking me if I've lost weight, even when I clearly haven't—you're a sweet and smart man; Julie Christiansen, Barbara Stotko and Melissa Paul for beta reading; Jedediah for putting up with my stress-ball ways while I got this done; my friends who rallied around me and gave me the support and affirmation I needed to finish. And a big thank you to The Apartment Manager's Blog readers—you've all been so encouraging throughout this entire journey, and I appreciate it so much.

About the Author

Erin Huss is a former on-site apartment manager and current blogger at The Apartment Manager's Blog—a chronicle of the comical (and often bizarre) accounts of property managers. Erin lives in Southern California with her husband, five children, two dogs, and lots and lots of fish.

Keep up with Erin online:

Newsletter: http://bit.ly/erinhussnews (and get *Can't Pay My Rent* for free—normally $2.99)
Website: TheApartmentManagersBlog.com
Facebook: TheApartmentManagersBlog
Twitter: @ErinHoganHuss
Instagram: ErinHuss
Email: ErinHuss@gmail.com

Other Titles by Erin Huss

Check out the rest of the Apartment Manager series:

For Rent, a romantic comedy about Cambria's struggles as an apartment manager.

Can't Pay My Rent, the original book of 31 real-life reasons why tenants claimed they couldn't pay their rent, free when you sign up for Erin's mailing list: http://bit.ly/erinhussnews (normally $2.99).

Still Can't Pay My Rent, the hilarious sequel to *Can't Pay My Rent* with 31 more real-life excuses for not paying the rent.

Move-In Special, a sequel to the popular romantic comedy *For Rent* (Coming 2017!)

Read on for a sneak peek of *For Rent*...

Excuses come in 31 flavors…
Can't Pay My Rent

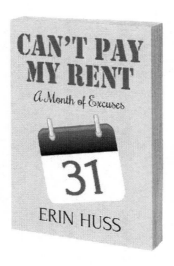

Why can't you pay the rent?

The monthly question most apartment managers find themselves asking at least a handful of tenants. In this hilarious piece, Cambria Clyne, the sassy heroine of *For Rent*, is presented with 31 real-life excuses for not paying the rent. Everything from "my identity was stolen" to "I needed drinking money for the weekend" is offered as a so-called reasonable attempt to get out of forking over the cash (or unsigned money order or check that will surely bounce).

Now the question is: How will Cambria get them all to pay up?

Get it for free! Sign up for Erin's newsletter, and she'll send you a free ebook of *Can't Pay My Rent*: http://bit.ly/erinhussnews

FOR RENT

The Apartment Manager Series

ERIN HUSS

velvet morning
press

Chapter 1

Seeking an on-site Apartment Property Manager for a charming 40-unit community. Applicant must have excellent organizational skills and a calming demeanor.

"Calm down!"

Honk.

"You're not the only one in a hurry."

Hooonk.

"Go around!"

The silver BMW roared past me. I turned to deliver a mad glare, but Captain Douche was too busy looking at his phone to notice.

"Pay attention to the road!" I yelled to his rear bumper. "Honestly, no one can drive in this city." I flipped down my visor. The zit in the middle of my freckled forehead pulsed in the tiny mirror. "You really couldn't have waited until tomorrow?" I asked the zit.

I reached over and grabbed my makeup bag, smothered the monstrosity in concealer, added a touch of gloss to my lips, and mascara'd my lashes into tiny tarantula legs. I had to look my best today. One more

week of unemployment and I'd be left with no other
option than to become a phone sex operator by night
who flips burgers by day. I had applications in for both
jobs in case this interview led to yet another dead end.

Hooonk!

"Take it easy." I flipped the visor back and continued
maneuvering my dented Civic through the crowded
streets of Los Angeles. I grabbed the past-due phone bill
out of my bag and double-checked the directions
scribbled on the back.

Right on City Court.

I looked up as the street sign for City Court drifted
by my window.

"Crap." I made a hasty U-turn, which inspired
another cacophony of horns. A man wearing a dirty
Spiderman costume weighed in on my poor driving
habits by flipping me a double-fisted bird. Even if I
didn't come *that* close to him or his overflowing grocery
cart.

My hand automatically went up as a feeble apology
before I made the sharp turn.

And there I saw it. An imposing ten-story building. A
cobblestoned walkway led up to a pair of whimsical
wrought-iron doors. Brilliant red and yellow flowers were
strategically dispersed throughout the lavish landscaping.
A sign, welcoming those who were clearly richer than me,
hung above a glistening koi pond near the entrance. It
was beautiful.

I parked under the sign pointing to the leasing office,
shoved the phone bill into my bag, and crawled over the
center console and passenger seat to exit the car. The
driver's side door had been stuck shut since an expensive
meeting with a runaway Dumpster a few months ago. It
was annoying and awkward, especially on the days when
I managed to squeeze my butt into a pair of skinny jeans.
My little Civic still managed to get me from point A to

point B (usually), and that was all I could afford to care about.

As I stepped onto the sidewalk, I flattened the front of my dress with my hands and brushed off the tiny crumbs clinging to my thighs. I had on an Anthropologie dress worth more than my car—the one designated for interviews and first dates only because it minimized my butt, elongated my waist, was dry clean only, and the navy color matched my eyes. Sadly, it hadn't been getting much action in the last—*oh let me see*—four years.

Rolling my shoulders back, I took a deep, calming breath. The irony that I was about to interview for a job as an apartment manager when I was nearing eviction from my own apartment was not lost on me. It had been six months since I was laid off. Finding a job when the qualifications portion of your résumé ran three deep wasn't easy. Neither was being a single mother. The phone call for this interview couldn't have come at a better time. Decent salary, apartment, utilities, medical benefits and bonuses—it was the perfect opportunity to get Lilly and me back on our feet. I only hoped my lack of apartment management experience would be overshadowed by my obvious desperation.

Setting my focus on the whimsical doors, I charged toward—*oomph!*

There was a step.

A big step.

A step I didn't see until my hands and knees were plastered atop the scorching cement, and I was staring at it.

"Are you OK?" A pencil thin tube top-donning brunette stood over me, sucking on a Tootsie Pop. Each boob popping out from her chest was bigger than my head.

"I think so." I peeled myself off the ground and brushed away the chalky debris coating my knees. "That step came out of nowhere."

The brunette flipped her long ponytail over her shoulder. "Yeah, it happens a lot. Like, that's why they put up the sign." She pointed her sucker to the caution sign with a person about to plunge to the ground like I had just done. "But it doesn't seem to help. I totally see people trip here, like, all the time."

"Do you live here?"

"Nope, my Boo lives next door."

"Next door? There's another apartment complex on this street?" Panicked, I checked my watch. The interview was scheduled to start in five minutes. Story of my life—I was never late. I was always *almost* late, enough to be a frazzled, sweaty mess when I did arrive.

She pointed her sucker toward a row of tall shrubs. "Yeah, it's over there."

"Crap... Thank you!" I yelled over my shoulder as I ran to the foliage fence blocking the neighboring apartment building. This one was smaller. Two-story with gated parking to the left. Pots filled with succulents lined the chipped brick walkway that led to a pair of sad-looking brown doors. No welcome sign. No koi pond, but a mud puddle near the entrance had a cloud of tiny insects hovering above it.

I dug out the instructions from my bag: *10, 405, Exit SM, Sepulveda, right on City Court. Apartment building on the right. Ask for Joyce.* That was it. That was all I wrote. No apartment name. No address. That would make too much sense.

I ran back to the first apartment complex. Standing between the two buildings, I shaded my eyes with my hand, trying to decide which one might house Joyce. The first building was much nicer. So I turned and ran toward the second one, because running toward mediocrity felt more natural.

When I reached the doors, I rested my hand on the

rusty knob. *You've got this,* I told myself. *You are a strong, confident woman with better-than-average abilities and a kid to feed.* I took another deep breath, pushed open the door and entered... 1988?

I blinked as my eyes adjusted to the pink-and-blue-striped wallpaper. A glass coffee table was surrounded by an overstuffed peach leather couch and two floral-printed armchairs. Below my Payless heels was teal carpet, followed by yellow linoleum with a repeating brown octagon pattern across it. The track lighting gave the room a yellowish, hazy tint, and a ceiling fan clinked with each turn of its golden blades, pushing the stale, nicotine-laced air around the ugly room.

To my right was an enclosed office with a waist-high counter (also teal) overlooking the lobby. A frail old woman with scarlet hair sat behind a desk, her hands clasped and brown eyes on me.

"Hi. Are you Joyce?" I asked, hoping she'd say no and direct me to the spa-like resort next door.

"I am," she answered in a barely audible rasp. Despite the hundred-degree outside temperature, she wore a sweater, which hung loosely around her bony frame. Just looking at the cashmere caused my sweat glands to produce in double time.

"I'm Cambria Clyne. I have an interview with Patrick for the apartment management position. His secretary told me to meet him here at noon."

"Hmm, *you* really want *this* job?"

What's that supposed to mean? "Yes, I do," I answered slowly.

She regarded me for several awkward seconds before speaking. "OK then. Up to you." She stood on shaky legs and shuffled up to the counter. The two-foot journey looked painful. "Nice to meet you, Cambria. I'm the current manager." I took her proffered hand. Her palm was cold, but her eyes had a hint of warmth to them.

"Patrick should be here in a bit. Would you like me to show you around while you wait?"

"That would be great, thank you." I smiled.

Joyce motioned for me to walk around the counter to the door that separated the lobby from the enclosed office. I followed her through the cramped space, squeezing past a row of tarnished filing cabinets and an L-shaped oak desk. She opened the door behind the desk and—BAM!

Find out what happens next... pick up your copy of *For Rent* today!

Got a vacancy on your bookshelf?
Check out the hilarious

Apartment Manager Series

35741294R00056

Made in the USA
Middletown, DE
13 October 2016